THE MIND'S OASIS

DREAMS AND EXPERIENCES

PANDURANGA RAO YELESWARAPU

Dedicated to my four daughters

Contents

Contents

Preface

Dreams come and disappear. The imprints only remain in the mind. How the dreams were formed and what they signify was beyond our comprehension. If the mind fails to capture the dream, it means that there was no dream. Dreams in a way were powerful and were a cause for surprise and could move a person. They cause pain, they cause pleasure. At times they give us happiness. and keep us cheerful. There appears to be no logical conclusions about the subject of dreams. How these dreams form was a miracle. It was for the dreamer to grasp the impressions and retain the experience if required by keeping a diary to refer later. The dream was only for the lonely person at that moment. There were no common dreams and there were no collective dreams.

Prologue

Pleasure and pain relate to physical and emotional environment of an individual's **Mind's Oasis** and is visible in the society. Happiness is personal and independent. It is purely connected to one's own intelligence and imagination. It remains as an integral part of solitude. External events are irrelevant to happiness. We can be happy, if we cultivate and aim at happiness. We become happiness. Wisdom lies in achievement of happiness.

ONE
GARBA DANCE

Dreams form in their own fashion. The formations were independent and unique by themselves.

On 24th September 2024, I saw in a dream a good number of people of "Yadav Community standing in circular formations. All were dressed in Yellow Dhotis and Kurtas. Their waists were tied by "Saffron coloured pieces of cloth. Their heads were tied and covered by White towels. Each one of them was holding a shining and well-polished sticks of One and Half Foot length in their hands. They were waiting for a sound to start their dance. These were boys and girls in the age group 12 and20 years.

Then I saw Sri Krishna in the middle of this group of dancers, standing with his flute in his folded hands. He started playing his flute. The entire group of dancers were electrified and started moving in circles, enchanted by the sound of the flute. Their hands were moving and playing with their neighbours' sticks making uniform rhythmic sounds. Their feet were thumping the ground. The formations were moving in circles. It was a sight worth witnessing.

I kept my distance from the movements. My entire attention was on Sri Krishna and the flute He was playing. I realized that the present day popular "Gharba "dances played during Dasara festivals, must have had their origins from their Originator Lord Sri Krishna and the Yadav community of girls and boys of bygone generation s. The beginnings must have had their seeds started growing at "Brindavan" on the shores of Narmada River.

If the dream could connect us to the origin of birth of "Garba" dances and Sri Krishna playing the flute; what a wonderful experience it was on 24TH September 2024. How powerful was the connectivity passing through countless generations. There were no boundaries nor any demarcations. Can anyone call it a wonder? Can there be such a dream recorded as an experience?

Honestly speaking there were certain things invisible to the naked eyes. There were certain things beyond the scope

Of our imagination, logic and reasoning. There were some things more authentic and creatively hidden in a human being. This uplifts his stature and capacity. This dream put me on a mat and became the cause for my inspiration. I decided to collect all the dreams I came across. I compiled the narratives given by others. In a way these narrations were disjointed, periodic gaps, time lags and the persons involved. Nevertheless, they were authentic and nearer to the truth.

After awakening and coming under the full control of the senses, I was unable to differ and distance myself from the experience of the dream. We were a split personality. We were a Tridimensionality personality. The basic reality, at fundamental level was our birth, in which we had nothing to choose, we were thrown on this planet, as a gift by Nature. The Second formation was shaped by the society in which we were brought up. We were nurtured, influenced by the social environment, a major piece of our existence. The Third piece comes from an unknown source of awareness. A Divinity of its own kind touching the senses, influencing the mind, leaving at that stage to form one's own impressions. It was not a gradual growth. It would occur at any time, any age to anyone. It could be Sri Gajendra struggling to free himself, Bhakta Prahalada trying to convince his father, Prince Dhruva to fulfil his desire to sit on the lap of his father, Bhakta Meerabai fully immersed in her devotional songs. It could be a reality, touching the body or mind or a dream influencing the future course of action. It could be for a short duration like the lightening in the sky or rainbow colours on the Sunshine rays after the rain. It was the individual's exposure to Divinity. It could be his own wealth his own Gold Mine, it was personal, and no one could be competent to share.

All these Three stages intermingle push the individual forward to conduct his voyage called life. The voyage continues under turbulent waters and rocky surfaces. They provided the immune system, strength for endurance. It could cut the threads at any time and close the life span once for all.

The choice to cope up with the life was given to the individual. Each one of us was separate by himself like the granules in the basket. The narration was based on this Trajectory.

Basing on this dream as a thrilling and authentic experience connecting Lord Sri Krishna, His youthful days, the cheerful gatherings of Yadav community of those days gave unparallel happiness. We, as individuals do not know from where the happiness comes, our duty was to grab it.

My friend, you might have had your own experiences unique to yourself. Enjoy the value of happiness stored in you.

TWO
TURN AROUND

The other day, a retired Chief Engineer, lamented "I am already 82 years old. Indeed, I am a sufficiently old person. Off late I developed pain in knee joint. Daily walking in the lawn becomes a nightmare exercise. A curse indeed!

These utterances stirred my imagination, as I was touching 90 years. I tried to look for a remedy. "After all, to live without hope, is cease to live ". I started the turnaround way, of the same dialogue "I am a man of 82 years of rich experience in life. I can easily roll another 5 years with pulsating energy and enthusiasm.

What options are at my disposal?

Play with grandchildren at regular intervals at their conveniences. This is a fine option and a good past time.

Taking care of my family which I was doing for the last 50 years and there was nothing new about it. It would go on for the next 5 years. No extra effort was needed.

I could plan seeing places of interest like a tourist, presuming my body would co-operate with minimum discomfort. If need be, I could take the help of a wheelchair. Every tour was one time effort, as we were not inclined to visit the same place twice.

I am financially sound, comparing with the neighbourhood. There was no hurry to further accumulate wealth.

What else.?.

I was indulging in a narrative way of thinking mood. To what extent a man could imagine extending his creative urge and scale new heights, instead of remaining static and lethargic. After all it could take Six months or so to assess and assemble the events of pain and pleasure of past decades. It would take another Three months to fine tune and polish the narratives. These would include the pains you thought were un-surmountable and the pleasures you thought should continue for some more time. Otherwise, time would slip away through your fingers without your knowledge. Leading a life of self-indulging routine manner like dry grass, anyone would walkover.

I came across a story of a person, who started learning alphabets at the age of 45 years. He used to take his son to the school in the morning and bring him back in the evening. He also joined the school and started learning. Within a span of 10 years, he developed mastery over Theosophy, which became his favourite subject. He started giving lectures on Theosophy and earned a name in the neighbourhood. To his misfortune, he was caught in a criminal case at the age of 90 years and was sentenced to undergo 5 years imprisonment. He used to collect the prison inmates and started conducting classes on Theosophy. At the age of 95 years, he breathed his last in the prison.

There was another episode of tenacity and endurance. Annual competitions were held every year in France, for producing the best "Tulip Flower" of the year. Many farmers were keen in competing and try their luck, in producing the best "Tulip Flower ". To produce the best "Tulip Flower "of competitive level one needs expertise, the proper Sunshades, moisture, protection from pesticides, night vigil etcetera.

There was a farmer who was a dedicated Tulip Flower grower. He had no other interest except producing the flower and participating in the "Annual Competition." for the prize. To his bad luck unfortunately he was caught in a criminal case and jailed. It was a great disappointment. His enthusiasm was crushed to the bottom level. He felt that Nature had no sympathy for him and his

hands were tied. He lost the hope of participating. He was kicking his heels in the prison day and night. He used to walk daily in the prison yard kicking the pebbles. He spent restless nights in the prison cell. As a part of his routine with down cast eyes he started walking in the yard kicking the pebbles. He was hundred meters away from his cell. Something soft struck his sole. He bent low and examined the soil. His eyes looked up and saw the Sun rays. His entire body was galvanized. He was convinced that it was the best soil to develop the Tulip plant. His enthusiasm leaped high and there was a smile on his face. He would develop the 'Tulip Flower" of his dreams. He contacted the prison warden convinced of his plans to grow the Tulip plant and if God willing, he would compete in the "Annual Competition". He collected all the tools, shading screens water cans, pesticides and plunged into the work whole heartedly. He forgot all the miseries of the prison cell.

He was like a mother nursing her newborn child. How to feed when to feed and how much to feed only the mother knows the best! Our farmer was at the plant with the shadow screens in the day and nighttime and protect the Plant growth, even in full moon nights he was at the plant site. The flower slowly blossomed in the prison yard the brainchild of our prisoner. He won the National Annual Award, for the best '" Tulip Flower" of the year.

What I intend to say was that there was immense capacity in an individual. How to explore was left to him and the society where he was living. We have the capacity to change, transform into a new "Avatar", shape the future for betterment irrespective of the pains we have undergone and the pleasures we shared with others.

I narrate a real story of our village, took place75 years ago. We had a boy in our village in the age group of 13/14 years. His name was "Pichaiah". Pichaiah means, a mad fellow. It was a belief to name children out of the normal way to ward off evil spirits and protect the children.

Pichaiah was notorious for stealing items in our village. In case any valuable item was lost or stolen the usual suspect was Pichaiah, People would rush to his house search and locate the item. His father would give him a good thrashing and put him back to the school. But the habit never left him. He was nick named as "Pichaiah, the village thief." During those days there were not many educational institutes. Children were forced to go to school as a routine habit.

One day Pichaiah was caught red handed while stealing a valuable item. People thronged to his house to beat him. His grandmother came to his rescue and supported his action. After all grandmothers were like that, full of affection. We all belong to the same village, connected by invisible threads of affections. All acquaintances see each other, and no one was a stranger in the village.

On that fateful day she shouted at everybody. She took name by name all the people and their grandfathers and how notorious and infamous they were, during their childhood. These revelations at the top of her voice put everybody on the mat. She washed the dirty linen and did not spare anyone.

Everyone was put to shame. Everyone one by one withdrew from the spot. We had the field day, and all the notorious acts of previous generation surfaced including the stealing of coconuts from the backyards of the houses.

During those days the emotional spirits were very high, since the Nation got Independence. Hindi was hailed as National Language. A good number of scholarships were offered to the students of Southern States, whoever was wishing to learn Hindi. Pichaiah of our village got the scholarships one after another. He climbed the ladder quickly and scaled the heights in Hindi Language. Pichaiah finally landed as a Professor of Hindi. He was appointed as Professor of Hindi and Head of the Department of Hindi Faulty at the University of Tiruvantapuram. The entire village was proud of this achievement. No one had the courage to call Pichaiah, the village thief.

Remaining stagnant within the physical frame as a lump of mud and refusing to grow is against human spirit and incorrect from all angles.

Never put God the Almighty as your defender. God is a Star for guidance. It is perpetual and the choice is yours. We want to be somebody other than what we were was the starting point of fear. The real producer and the wholesale seller of this commodity called Fear was the Society at large from top to bottom. By observing our own actions, we could know how foolishly we try to appease others.

We were wise, we were intelligent, we have the qualifications and we were well paid. But some people were not knowing what integrity was. All the infamous scams relate to lack of integrity. Looking at the voluminous society, we could only try to improve and change our individual self and not the society at large.

THREE
FESTIVAL

Lord Ganesha's festival was celebrated in every Hindu family at their residences. This year it was falling on 7th September 2024. People would affectionately invite each other to visit their homes and pay tributes to Lord Ganesha installed at their residences. This customary gesture developed into a respectable and compulsory obligation. People invariably attend their close relations and friends' houses. Over the years it became a family get together and exchange of greetings. These courtesies would go on till the last day of immersion and farewell to Lord Ganesha.

I reproduce the WhatsApp message received from my old friend in the evening of 7th September 2024. No additions no subtractions.

"We often behave strangely in our relationships with our kith and kin and other family members. Age was no bar. All my daughters crossed above 42 years of age and were looking after their own families. You were aware I was touching 90 years.

I took a sudden and rash decision to leave my daughter's home and never to return. It was on 2nd September 2024.around 10' o clock .in the morning. Lord Ganesha's festival was falling on 7th September 2024.There would be full fanfare in every house. In fact, I arrived at their residence some 13 years back after completing 75 years of age. I was looking after their welfare and my security considering my age factor. I was content with my routine.

Of late I developed a feeling that my daughter was adopting an insulting tone considered not conducive in a family relationship. The behavioral pattern was not palatable to me. I had to spend my time as a non-entity at their residence. I was like a drifting log floating in a river. I was an unavoidable liability.

I was slowly slipping into frustration and equally annoyed with her visible tantrums. Sometimes there was friction. I resorted and indulged in scolding her for her temperamental behaviour. At times I used to go away to the nearby temple towns for a stay of 3 to 4 days. It was more a pretence than devotion. No one in the house had the inkling of the pattern of my behaviour. It was taken for granted that my visits were for pilgrimage and not as escape routes.

My daughter lost that soft touch of affection belonging to a father in the usual manner. It was visible on the surface. The invisible affectionate threads supposed to exist in a closed family circle were slowly disappearing. She was adamant and exhibiting lot of hatred for no fault of mine. I slowly started withdrawing and maintaining distance within the house. Even a small sound made while placing the glass on the table was irritating her. Why I was hated, why these repulsions honestly, I had no idea. I went on reflecting on my status and why I was not able to conduct smoothly myself. Why so many speed breakers at small distances.

What would happen if I, once for all retreat. Where to go and where to stay? What were my options? What others would think of my behaviour? These were big questions! But hatred was a bigger hurdle to cross. At the same time, it was difficult to swallow the poison. It was always easy to preach morals, standing at the seashore. Any person moving in the society could utter morals, easily and without any hesitation, so long the waves were not touching his feet.

The question was how to keep myself in balance. What would happen to myself image at this age? Human being was really a strange animal. He had no fixed pattern of behaviour like other animals. Even a request for a railway reservation on "Laptop "sitting at home was point blank rejected. I was told to go to Railway Reservation Counter and do it myself at the station. It was an insult to my stature. You know very well I was a retired Class I Officer of Central Government I had the experience of moving in different offices. Never I was at loggerheads with any other human being. Going to a Reservation Counter was not a big deal. Even an illiterate person was helped at the Counter to get his reservation.

I was undergoing an inescapable frustration in the Heart. There was no escape and no remedy. We were behaving like strangers in a sleeper coach searching for our berth numbers. I was fully aware that the decision to leave their house was out of frustration and disappointment in the surroundings. Forty years of nourishment and affection towards a daughter had no value and meaning when it comes to unpredictable behaviour.

I informed my daughter that I was leaving her younger sister's house once for all. I was going to the Reservation Counter to make reservation to an unknown destination. I was not inclined to tell my son-in Law about quitting their house and not returning afterwards. In any case my daughter would tell him. My other daughter advised me not to precipitate matters and proceed. We would discuss and settle amicably. I did not want to visit her home as a refugee. I told her that I was not coming to Mumbai. I dashed out and was proceeding towards the Lift. In the meantime, I received the printout of the reservation ticket for my visit to Mumbai. I thought stretching too far was not wisdom. Once the thread was broken the knot would remain forever. The smoothness of the thread would be missing. I made a "U Tern" and reached Mumbai on 04.09.2024.

On 5th my daughter from Bengaluru telephoned me. She conveyed that she was sorry for hurting my feelings. She sincerely felt that her temperament was not correct. She should be given a Second chance to mend her ways. I had no desire to hurt anyone's feelings nor hate anyone. I was not cynical in my attitude. Worst comes worst it would be always a search for escape route in all dealings of my life.

After all a daughter was a daughter. It was a Nature's gift. Parents were not requested to express their choice. One had to accept the gift as it was delivered. I was blunt and reluctant to concede to her request. A person would not reflect on his own emotions, however best he would try. They were like flood gates. The waters must move. The pressures must decrease, and the waters choose its own way. Human beings were in no way different from these waters. I informed my daughter that right or wrong it was my decision. No one need to share the blame. The wheels had to move. I told her how bad I was feeling. Hatred was a poison. It would only harm and never solve any problem. No one was ever willingly to swallow it. It was immaterial from which angle it was served. Lord Ganesha could only solve predicament I was facing.

On 7th September 2024, the festival starting day I was suffering with back pain and needed rest. My daughter at Mumbai made all the decorations and gave a call to all of us to come and join the pooja. Lord's pooja was about to start. Reluctantly I responded "Yes. I am coming. I was on the bed and slowly started sleeping. In the meantime, someone was shouting that my 4th daughter came from Bangaluru. There was no prior intimation. I thought, presumably she came by plane. I saw her in full form standing at the entrance to the hall. I got up, took hold of her hand and proceeded into the hall and from there nearer to Pooja Mandir. I dragged a chair told her to sit and participate in Pooja along with her sister. No one was aware of her presence, except me because it was all in the dream.

I felt it was Lord Ganesha who brought my daughter all the way from Bengaluru to Mumbai. Her presence opened my eyes. In few minutes all my resentment was wiped out. The logic, reasoning, and the intelligence of the mind including the reservations I had, were all disappeared. I was convinced that mind had no business when it comes to Lord Ganesha and His way of dissolving the conflicts in any situation. Lord Ganesha elevated my status of understanding and my erratic behaviour as if it never occurred. In His presence who was right who was wrong gets submerged and everything submerged in worship. They disappear in no time, only affections remain.

God was all powerful. All Souls bend and obey Him. With Him all was well, and no human intelligence stands in the way. There were no contradictions in His love, it was welfare only. I did not feel guilty for any of my recent failures. I had a good number of failures in the past. One more addition did not make any difference.

My daughter: Never hate anybody. It would never give good results.

Stop hating. I was put in the dock without affections. The worst foolish act for anyone was hatred. I could see you in physical form without your actual presence, was purity. Only Lord Ganesha had put our affections on right path.

FOUR
OH—MY DAD...

I heard you were collecting the episodes for your compilation. It was a thrill at the age of 90 years. I am sending a piece of my experiences for consideration if you deem it worthy for inclusion. I assure you that they were authentic, factual and nearer to truth if not100% but more than 90%.

I was always a timid person in front of my father. The timidity might have entered from childhood. It remained with me throughout my life, even after the demise of my father 32 years back. One had to live with it and no escape was possible. I would confirm this characteristic of main with the dream that occurred in the afternoon. I was resting on a cot. The atmosphere was cool, it was cloudy, the weather was refreshing and energetic. That was the specialty of Bengaluru. I was not aware when I was dragged into sleep. Suddenly the surroundings changed. I saw my father standing near a hot pan and preparing a Dosa. He was mending it with the Dosa handle. I went nearer to him and asked, why he was preparing Dosa all alone as if there was no one at home. I took the handle from his hand and started mending it. I felt miserable that we have ignored Daddy when we were celebrating "Get Together Function" on 28th April 2023. I felt that the Soul was unhappy and expressed its displeasure and disappointment like any other human being. When this thought entered my mind and my Heart, I felt the agony and tears started rolling from my eyes, Nearby I also saw my elder brother standing by the side of my father in white paint and white shirt. He also expired 5 years back. The dream dissolved and I looked at the wall clock. It was 12.15 afternoon.

I decided to do Anna Dana in my father's name to appease the Soul. The very next day I went to the nearby temple and made arrangements for Anna Dana giving our Gotra and my father's name.

I felt relieved. It was a rare experience.

Recently I had another dream. My father was riding a cycle. He was wearing a" T Shirt' of Olive Green colour well ironed. I had no idea from where he bought the T- Shirt. T-Shirts were not the fashion during his days. It was always full shirt with sleeves and buttons. Even while attending wedding ceremonies, it was the standard dress.

My father was energetic with a fresh countenance and a smile. It was the same face I could easily recall whenever we visited his working station during our summer vacations. We visited "Ganga Khed" a village on the banks of "Godavari River". The railway bridge across the river was at an elevated height. Jumping from there into the river waters below was a chivalrous act at our age. While the passenger train, crossing the bridge people used to through coins of "Nizam State" currency called "Haali"as a mark of worship to Mother Godavari.

It was a real pleasure to inhale a deep breath, holding it in the lungs, dive deeply into the waters reach the sandy floor, search for the coins through our little fingers. It was a real sport. With several dips, we used to collect around 15 or so coins almost equal to a rupee. It was a thrilling experience after the train crossed the bridge. There was a smiling face on each one of us for the Collection of coins. It was a real sport for every one of the boys. We used to share the coins with the local villagers. Those were the pleasant moments of our childhood life.

During that period "Ganga Khade" and the adjacent villages were attacked by "Plague" a contagious disease spread by the rats. The entire village was vacated. People used to cook their meals on the banks of the river "Godavari" and sleep there in the nights. We were in the railway quarters nearer to the station. We had a big buffalo and a calf. Both were robust to look at. My mother used to churn the curd in a big earthen pot, collect the butter and distribute the butter milk to the villagers. I could recall my father carrying his duties at the railway station. It was the same face without any anxiety, without any fear and tension.

On another Summer vacation we landed at a roadside railway station "Manvath Road ". The town ship was away from the railway station. The town had a cinema hall, and my father used to take us for a picture now and then. It was in1948 AD, The Razakar movement was at its peak. Local Hindu population were very much afraid. Those were very painful days. The Nizam was the ruler. The police were to maintain the Law and Order. The Razakars were the Third layer of authority not accountable to any law and order. In a way they were functioning like a local ruffian group. The police were closing their eyes or looking other way. The Razakars would exercise their authority, loot, plunder as they wish and enjoy the fallouts. They were functioning like local jaghirdars. The local people though in majority had to suffer all the indignities and no place to go. It was the same situation in all the districts of Nizam State.

We were children in the age group of 10 to 12. There was no place to go except the railway platform. After the train left the platform the cinema owner used to visit the station to collect his tin box containing the cinema reels. He was a prominent local Razakar of the town. He used to converse with my father, both being in the same age group. The cinema hall owner, as a sportive gesture used to remove the "Khanger "(an Urdu word for a dagger) from the lather sheath, laughingly pointing it at my father's stomach and say "Arh, Mansterji one day it would pierce your stomach." My father used to reply; Arhe, Sahib, I saw a good number of Khangers in my life. Who cares for it? It was a routine affair whenever he used to visit the station to collect his tin box. I recollect that face of my father, without fear, not moving an inch from where he was standing in his uniform.

One day my father received a panic message that the local Razakars were planning to wipeout our entire family in the night.

The train was ready to leave the Manvath Road station platform, proceed to Manmad via Aurangabad a notorious Razakar bastain. My father came to our railway quarters. He told us "Run and catch the train". We bundled our cloths and ran to catch the train. We entered the compartment and sat at the door. A few benches were empty. But we were afraid to sit there thinking that the Razakars would get offended and react vehemently. The steam engine started moving slowly with its creeping sound. My father bade us farewell, standing near the door. There were tears in our eyes including my mother. But there was no change in my father's face. The train gained movement, and the distance increased. After Four hours travel, we reached Manmad, a safe place for Hindus. I still remember my tears and the hand stretched through the window to reach my father. There was no worry, no tears, not even a moisture in the eyes of my father's face. That was my daddy!

I saw the same face which was standing on the platform of "Manvat Road, after 75 years in my dream.

A fearless face was always blessing and a gift of Nature. Slowly we interact in the society, become pragmatic down to Earth and at times whimsical. In my dream, I felt that the Atma was fully satisfied with the "Annndanam. We offered the Annadanam on 8ᵗʰ July 2024. The Soul came back after 51 days and conveyed its greetings. I had no knowledge of how the prayer of Annadanam had travelled and reached the intended Soul. The Soul came back cheerfully and gave its blessings. I was happy when I woke up from the dream. I still accept that I was a timid fellow in front of my DADDY.

FIVE
SOLITUDE-ATTITUDE

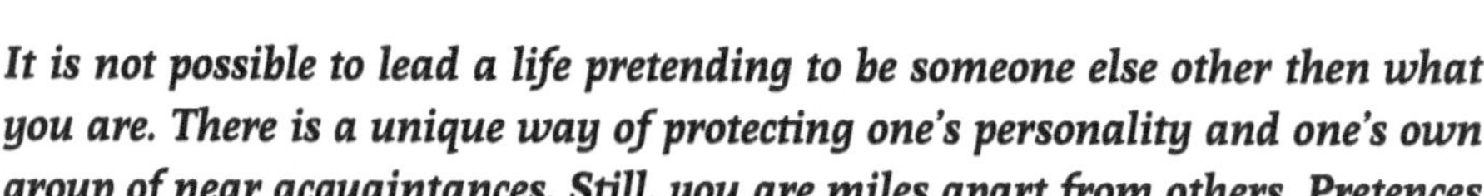

It is not possible to lead a life pretending to be someone else other then what you are. There is a unique way of protecting one's personality and one's own group of near acquaintances. Still, you are miles apart from others. Pretences are acceptance of defeat (Abraham Lincon).

"A common saying" You can fool all the people for some time, some of the people all the time, but not all the people all the time." But ignorance also keeps a person cheerful despite all the advanced age. For example, what makes you happy is a big question for the rest of your life? These are all related to attitudes and frequently alter their focus as the pressures mount. Attitude cannot be a constant companion.

Let us quote the historic meeting of Alexander the Great, The Emperor, and the Greek Philosopher named "Diogenes ", who lived in a giant base on the streets of "Sinope".

He thought nothing of begging for food nor ashamed of it. For Alexander, The Great, happiness means conquering the lands best food best decorative clothes, wealth, increasing power, court gestures all around.

Diogenes on the other hand, believed that happiness lies in solitude, simplicity an attitude free from the constant struggle acquiring wealth and power.

When Alexander the Emperor want to offer Diogenes, good food, good clothing pearls and gold coins, Diogenes snapped back to everyone's astonishment. He said to Alexander, The Great Emperor, "Move over. I am enjoying the sunshine. Do not block it with your shadow"

The emperor was shattered and shocked. Later, he was heard saying "If I were not the Alexander the Great, I would be happy to be Diogenes".

Years later his death bed at the age of 32 years, Alexander was said to have made three declarations (death wishes), the second one was as under.

"When my coffin was being carried to the grave, Let the entire path leading to the graveyard be strewn with the wealth, gems, diamonds, pearls that I have conquered. Let the world know that the Alexander the Emperor could not carry even a farthing with him. Ultimately all these wealth would turn to dust like my body".

Nothing worthwhile had ever been attained without sacrificing some comfort. This includes those who lost themselves in despair. Instead of preparing to be happy let us be happy today. Let not anything disturb our happiness on this day.

Incidents do take place unknowingly. In a large society we cannot avoid them. One evening there was a phone call around 7.00 PM, call from The Assistant station master "One elderly person around 85 years of age was loitering on the Platform. Other than Telugu he was not knowing any Language", I was called to the station to help this elderly person. I went talked to him in Telugu. I invited him to our railway quarter, which was nearby, I made him comfortable. My wife cooked food. There after he went to bed and slept.

He did not reveal much about his expedition. I also left it at that level, thinking that in the morning I would enquire and settle the matters to the best of my ability and to the best of his attitude. In the morning my wife went to him and requested the elderly person to brush his teeth, and she would bring a cup of coffee. There was no movement and no response. My wife alarmingly called me, and I approached the bed. The elderly person might have died during the sleep. We were not knowing his identification. The news was spread like current and all the collected in no time. One person was knowing the Circle Inspector. We informed him about what took place in our quarter. The Circle Inspector said collect ten Thousand rupees for any eventuality. He would send the police. The police come and conducted "Panchanama". They took our statements; The baggage was searched. We were asked to calm down.

The police informed the sons who were at Chennai. The eldest son comes by the plane. He gave statement that they were not suspecting any foul play. Their father was in the habit of leaving the house without informing any one whenever he was annoyed and angry with the members of the household. Arrangements were made to lift and take the body by van to Chennai.

The nightmare was over. We took an oath not to indulge in philanthropic acts and invite troubles at our doorsteps. It was a lesson for a lifetime that pragmatism rules over philanthropy.

Coming back to the basic theme, solitude was to be cultivated nurtured to understand the virtues of solitude. Without determination one cannot gain momentum in his attitude. What was visible was the only starting point for gaining wisdom and its uninterrupted growth. The multidimension growth would occur by stirring the imagination. The universal truth was we need a mob or a crowd to celebrate pleasure or a gathering to clap. But real happiness comes from solitude and from within one's own self and not from outside sources. Solitude was an attitude of the mind. These were to be compulsorily generated by the individual and not by a mob contact. These were depending on our thoughts, the methods we cultivate and the habits we nourish and adopt them in our system. I assure you happiness lies in solitude.

Once in a dream I saw in the early hours of the morning, an allegory was flowing down in a water wall. It was looking at me and started moving slowly in my direction. I became panic and started climbing upwards against the current of the water flow. In any case the creature was far away. I was struggling to climb and was slipping and unable to climb the heights. The creature took short cuts and was almost behind my back. You could imagine the horror I was facing. Finally with a commanding nerve I could come out of the slippery waters, climbed the rock. I was on a dry ground. I escaped the brutal attack of the reptile. It was like a war between the animal and a man, a victim of circumstances but intelligent enough to overcome the danger. This was built in the immune system of our body. A reptile a poisonous snake or a harmful creature seen in dream was a sure sign of impending disease. We can even make out which part of our body was going to be affected. Finally, the dream and the fear it generated had disappeared.

Talent is a product an individual creates by himself and not a gift by his neighbour. Conceive an idea, pursue it whole heartedly. It would take a shape to your satisfaction. Freedom is far more rewarding than slavery and taking orders. While crossing the street never trust the judgement of the drivers of other vehicles. They might not stop the vehicles for your movements and for your safety.

I give an incident quoted in the News paper. Two friends were moving on a motorcycle. They were cutting jokes moving erratically and were not allowing any vehicles to overtake them. It went on for 100 meters. The driver horning from behind had no effect on these guys. Finally, they moved ahead, hackling the car driver "Sorry Brother". The fellow was offended and followed the motorcycle riders for 100 meters found a gap and dashed from behind.

The fellow sitting behind fell and died. The rider also fell and was injured. It was a dog pursuing another dog. Who had the best interest in you other than yourself. Even between a man and a woman the relationship was most of the time lust and not love. Do not fool yourself. Nothing lasts forever.

There was a retired pilot officer who wanted a divorce from his wife. He was 89 years old, and his wife was not dragging behind with 85 years. The case getting adjourned for a very long period. The wife argued before the judge that she had no grievance against her husband. She would look after him very well. She had no objection for the divorce. But she never wanted to die as a divorcee. The judge understood her emotions and respected her feelings. The divorce case was rejected.

The relationships were how we were related to each other. It could be a relationship between wife and husband, it could be between two brothers or between friends, to whom we were related was immaterial and how close was the relationship. Everyone desires a long-lasting relationship a faithful relationship. Pretence was not a relationship though it looks like connected at surface value. There might be an influencing factor. We generally would not doubt a relationship, till we were deceived outright. The duration was not a material factor.

In our village there were two brothers. The elder brother was blind. The younger brother used to take him to our village canal with the help of a stick, bath him and bring him back to home. One day the elder brother fell into the canal and was washed away in the current and died. All the village people came and consoled the younger brother, and it was a difficult task. Slowly after some time there was a change in the behaviour pattern of the younger brother. He was spending money lavishly and indulging in erratic habits. The villagers started doubting his credentials. Was his brother's death being really an accident or a wilful act to get rid of him. But the riddle was not solved. Even after a decade the stigma remained as a rumour in our village. Unless we investigate the pattern of behaviour, we would not be able to conclude how sacred was the relationship and how best it was nourished.

God alone was the witness!

SIX
FREEDOM OF CHOICE

We possess the freedom of choice and will power to exercise, unlike the wild animals of the forest. Throughout its life, the animals have only one unified direction. They kill and devour the prey and feed their bellies. Nothing distracts their attention. They hunt for the prey throughout their life. That was the aim, that was the purpose, and that was the end of their life.

Human beings on the other hand have a purpose, capacity to change their aims, foresight to look into the future. They think of adopting new strategies, to scale new heights. The latest craze for towers in the cities was in this direction. Remaining stagnant, lethargic within the physical frame and not struggling to improve their intelligence, it was not a life designated for human beings. The progress made one generation after another was the abundant proof. Fear of the stranger, too much ambition and stress developed for security and safety created occasional wars among kings and nations, were the main killers in humans,

The present generation with all the intelligence at its command were still struggling to come out of this predicament. The information is bombarded from all the corners of the Globe. But what an individual could do collecting so much information and making his mind like a workshop. The emphasis should be on selection of choices and not on collection of information. What was the use of collecting the information about an individual when he constantly changing his behavior. Analytical study was based on Mathematical approach and could be used for conducting functions of the society. Lateral thinking was always for solving the problems faced by the individual and remains original. There cannot be a common and uniform solution. It was not based on traditional or known methods. It must be on innovation. Illogical way of thinking never solved any problem in the past nor it would be in future. It. only results in more complications.

A man should not feel guilty of any of his recent failures, because he must have faced bigger failures in the past decades. One should rather flush out poor thoughts and fill them with good thoughts. We worry about past events, about which we could do nothing. We equally worry about future uncertainty which always create doubts in our minds.

I narrate a behavioral pattern of an individual who retired from service. To his misfortune he became a victim of Parkinson's disease. He refused to accept that he had retired from service. In the morning, he would take bath, dress up neatly, sit and eat breakfast, take hold of his briefcase (That was a habitual weight for all office goers). He would reach the station for the local train in time. He would occupy a window seat. After all he had to reach Chatrapati Shivaji Terminus. In the evening, he would reach home as usual, as if he had attended office. His wife used to enquire where he had been loitering all day. His standard reply was there plenty of work in the office. We used to make fun of him. Why was he going to office? After all he had retired. If he sits at home the local window seat would be useful to somebody. But he was present for all the Five days of a week without fail.

Everyone could do something creative, because Nature had equipped us that way. In addition, to this our internal immune system could with stand for Eighty years unless we willfully spoil it with our compulsive habits. These were socially created habits but were not gifted by Nature.

Our creative urge remains dormant under the phobias and the weight of the yokes put on our necks and forced us to pull the loads. The Authorities created the yokes of different sizes to run the society and safeguard its safety and security. We as members of the society were obliged to pull the loads. The situations would always be a carrot and a whip.

Some of the brilliant people failed in life as per social standards. They were not knowing that the society only pays wages for the services rendered and not for what one knows. We were accustomed to see the light as white the only color. All the other colors were hidden within the white color. Unless we disaffirm them, we would not know the number of colors hidden in it. Likewise, deep within a man there lies a good number of talents, hidden sources of strengths and powerful combinations. Once revelations come to surface, we would be astonished. We could quote the example of Eakalavya

Self Esteem is a belief that we deserve to be happy and success full in life. We become successful when we understand that failure is an event and never a person. Accept that you are a beautiful person, refuse to accept others verdict.

After all our personalities were Nature's gift and not a society's verdict. Opting out was not a solution. But several persons opt out. Most people spend 90% of the time in defending their point of view instead of knowing the truth. Selfishness was a standard norm deeply rooted for survival in the society. We uphold rational selfishness was an acceptable norm, whatever it conveys. I quote an example. The nephew of a powerful person in Government hierarchy, approached the factory manager convinced him of bulky Purchase Order for his product. He collected an advance of Rs. 80lakhs, for processing the Purchase Order. In a routine check-up at railway platform, he was caught with his suitcase. He could not give any proper explanation for cash of Rs. 80 lakhs. The cash was confiscated, and the nephew was put behind bars.

We conceive the idea of deceiving of deceiving somebody with full confidence, but at times it fires back. The further consequences may not fully happen as per our planning. Any person can live peacefully, lovingly without stress and anxiety for the day till Sun Set. This is what the life really means. Every day was a new life for a wise man. Common sense reminds us that worry was not taking us anywhere. Worry destroys our ability to concentrate. Worry usually disappears in the light of the knowledge. Emotions of fear hatred, jealousy, envy were developed in the interactions between individuals in the society. They relate to the dynamics of the forest. There was no place for such dynamics in a welfare state, where people prefer independence. In freedom we were occupied in doing constructive and creative work,

"I would lose in action, lest I wither away in despair" This saying would appeal even to Indra-The Lord of heaven. Without purpose days would end in disintegration. The secret of being miserable was to bother about whether we were happy or not. Worry becomes a habit in small things, trivial matters magnified. I quote an incident. Long back a criminal was to be executed. He had a painful boil on his neck. The criminal was not pleading for his life. He requested the executioner not to hit on the boil with the axe because it was giving him a lot of pain already.

Knowledge became the basis for human welfare and progress. Research and invention related to Nature. The secrets s hidden therein and useful for further strengthening the welfare of humans must be explored by human effort. A good number of Scientific research had uplifted the humanity to greater heights. Splitting the Atom created nuclear energy Now the Solar energy was directly channeled through Solar panels. Satellites and spaceships, exploring whether Mars Planet was having water or not were all, the indications of human progress. In fact, our security welfare comforts have come out of our intelligence. Different people thought in different angles resulting in human progress. Knowledge became available to every seeker. Society was transforming into a global village very fast. We were left alone as dependent individuals. Interdependence was getting reduced. From a child to an Octogerian the pulse of freedom was visible. Pleasure and pain were reduced to personal level. When it comes to pain we were left alone. With pleasure we need at least Two to clap. One must balance both pain and pleasure knowing fully well that they belong to a temporary phase. Pain might be on account of ill health, terminal disease, injuries to the body. It was also on account of humiliation, loss of status defeat and poverty. On the other hand, pleasure was at irregular intervals and always welcome. It needs a minimum of Two individuals. Even clapping of hands give pleasure.

I was at a lodge restless worried by the pain caused on account of a boil on the thumb. It looked like a trifle when compared to the lodge cleaner who lost his forearm was doing all the chorus of the work in the lodge like filling the tank with water, cleaning the floors, cutting jokes with the inmates of the lodge. Always co-operate with the inevitable. Hellen Keller said "Keep your face towards Sunshine, you cannot see the shadow. Success is how high you bounce back when you hit the ground. General Patton the famous Second World Hero said "Being defeated, is often a temporary condition. Giving in what makes it permanent."

A daddy's boy! The teacher asked the student "Who had signed the America's Declaration of Independence? Pat came the student's reply. I do not know. I do not care! The teacher called the parent and complained about the rude behavior of his son. The father sternly looked at his son and said "You must tell the truth. If you have signed, admit it."

Anger, pride, deceit, greed arises out of selfish attitudes which stimulates and harm others. Self-awareness, ability to think about once own thought process enables one to stand apart, examine the way he sees himself.

Two saintly persons were vigorously engrossed in meditation. They were sitting under the shade of a "Tamarind Tree" We know the branches of Tamarin Tree were comparatively stronger, but the leaves attached to the rims were small and plenty. One day God appeared before one saint and asked "What for you are meditating? The saint replied, "I want to have Darshan of the Almighty." The God said "It is not that difficult. You please count all the leaves of this Tamarind Tree and do as many years as possible of meditation. Then God would appear in front of you." The saint was disappointed and depressed. The saint replied, "Sir It is a very difficult task, and the leaves are plenty and small to count," God disappeared. Next day God reappeared before the other saint and asked him "What for you are meditating? The saint replied "Sir I want to have the Darshan of the Almighty "The God said "It is very difficult to have the Darshan of the God. You must count the leaves of this Tamarin Tree and do meditation for as many years." The saint replied cheerfully "Is it so simple! Now itself I will start counting! Afterall attitudes count our actions.

Viktor Frankle was a prisoner in the "Death Camps of Nazi Government." His entire family perished except one sister. He himself was tortured suffered innumerable indignities, never knowing what would happen to him, the very next hour. For all the incidents occurring to an individual, he observed that self-awareness was a fundamental principle about the nature of the man. Our great power was our freedom to choose. Human being 's will be very powerful. Hellen Keller was a classic example. Willpower develops integrity. Integrity was the value one places on himself. There was no friendship without confidence. No confidence without integrity.

I give an example. Thirty y years of ethnic hatred resulting in civil war killing 120000 people in Sri Lanka. There was a tremendous power of conditioning and hatred as the children grew under such environment. Two rulers were at the helm of the affairs. They were unable to reconcile and solve the conflict for thirty years. They went on destroying the dwelling places schools' infrastructures. All powerful Nations remained as mere spectators. The same was being repeated between Ukraine and Russia, the war was there for the last Three years. Many families were destroyed and displaced. There was no count. Or there were no persons to take the count.

Even powerful leaders were counting their gains in terms of destroying the opponents' bridges, dwelling places, logistics. Even between Two individuals this hatred was visible though they were in no way concerned.

We had Two technicians coming from different continents to work for a project placed in a Third continent. We were all in a Team selected by "UNESCO" project. To the best of my knowledge in our Team in the case of these Two technicians, even their parents never visited Sri Lanka. It was quite possible that their great grandparents might have settled in Sri Lanka as Rubber Plantation Labor during Colonial period some 400 years back. In the case of our Two Technicians, one's Mother Tongue was Tamil and the other Technician 's happened to be Sri Lanka Language. None of us could speak in our Mother Tongue. We must communicate in English and no other choice. The day we landed asa Team 2000 kms away from Sri Lanka, these Two

Technicians were hating each other. It was visible clearly to us. The only reason for their mutual hatred was the Civil War that was going in Sri Lanka. Our values were so weak and harmful to each other despite our education and moving to distant places for livelihood. How silly was our superfluous way of forming opinions without any rationale, logic and reasoning.

I give another funny case. The judge in a divorce case passed the decree that the sale proceeds of his assets, the husband should share 50:50 % with his ex-wife. The husband started selling his assets at a throw away price and shared the proceeds 50:50. For example a car valued 10000 dollars he sold it for 200 dollars and gave 100 dollars to the ex-wife. This trend was not palatable to the ex-wife. She complained to The Court. The Court clerk verified and found the complaint was justified. The husband was conducting all the sales in the same manner. After all, when no one ever wins, perhaps being a looser was not that bad.

Unknowingly we were trapped into the emotional deep well, the waters of which were not visible even if we bend try to see the waters. Even well-educated people fall in this trap called "Emotional Hatred "This behaviour belongs to jungle Law, where hatred was ferocious. These people do not see they were living in a welfare society. We feel betrayed by these invisible forces.

The crisis between "UKRAINE AND RUSSIA" could have been handled in a better way instead of resorting to the power of weapons. Killing Thousands of people, displacing equal number of people destroying their houses, making them to run for a piece of bread is inhuman. Any amount of oratory would not justify the killing innocent people.

SEVEN
HAPPINESS

Happiness was a choice one should make for himself. Let it be for today or tomorrow, or thereafter. I prefer solitude. I do not want to be like an angry child of ego temperament willing to knockout the whole tower of blocks, because he was notable to balance One or Two blocks at the top. Happiness was not an external subject like pleasure and therefore there were no external solutions to gather happiness.

Touching 90 years of age what we desire most in a nutshell was happiness wholesale. I would prefer to collect and unify my thoughts to be happy. I would be rather happy than being right in my conduct and behavior. I would be happy wherever I am, this includes hospital bed. I would follow my preferences peacefully whether right or wrong. My interpretations of life were my own creations my own world and my own existence. That was happiness.

Recently I came across a gentleman standing always near a window looking outside for Thirty minutes daily in the morning and in the evening. The male nurse used to help him standing by his side. I was in the hospital bed nearby. The gentleman used to laugh now and then during interval s. Observing him daily, it slowly became a habit for me unknowingly and I also stared smiling and joined the chorus. Why I was also laughing I had no idea. For me as well as for him! After some days he stopped coming near to the window. His hospital bed remained vacant. I enquired from the male nurse, "What had happened to this gentleman.? Why was he not coming? The nurse replied "Sir, He was no more." As a mark of respect sympathy and pity for the victim I said" Poor fellow, he was missing the Nature he was enjoying daily standing at the window." The nurse replied" Sir, you were mistaken. He was blind. It was his habit of enjoying happiness. "

Happiness was a choice one should make for himself. Let it be for today, for tomorrow or next 5 years. I refused to accommodate myself in a "Old Age Homes "I prefer solitude" I never wanted to be an angry child of ego temperament, willing to knockout the whole tower of the blocks because I was not able to balance one or Two blocksat the top. Happiness was not an external subject like pleasure. Therefore, there were no external solutions, to invite happiness.

I refuse to recollect all the betrayals deceptions, infidelities occurred in the past that agonized me and troubled me to disturb my happiness and peace of mind in future. They were not of any significance for tomorrow and thereafter. Because nothing was unsurmountable except to death. Life often takes unexpected "U-Turns". Sometimes the results would cause enormous upheavals. People lose their mental balance. Sometimes collective hatred gains "Sunami "strength resulting in destruction of life and shelter. Who was responsible for the wildfire. No answers. Instead of fanning the flames the situation could be handled in a better way. To leave the world permanently was painful.

Meditation and prayers were helpful to reduce emotional loneliness. At the height of suffering Jesus Christ cried finally to the Almighty "Why this to me, why this to me". Let us therefore remain nearer to the loved ones. Happiness was a state of wellbeing with the natural push for its continuance. But it never happens that way. The only day we could call our day was today. The happiness we experience internally cannot be postponed for tomorrow or thereafter.

I recall an incident occurred in1982 AD. My grandmother went into coma and recovered after Seven days. She narrated "During those Seven days I was holding the photo frame of Lord Rama's coronation at Ayodhya. Death was after me threatening me to leave the photo frame. I refused and holding to my heart, even while taking bath at our village canal. Death was vexed and finally scolded me and left." I call it meditation and prayer. There were no full stops in life. We come across camas and semicolons. The full stop comes only once in a lifetime. We call it as death.

There was a calm and silence at the centre of our life. A very deep well with a crystal-clear water of happiness, that cannot be emptied. It could only be experienced. On the contrary our perceptions were twisted with doubts. Nothing goes according to our wishes. With tears and helplessness, we gather at the funerals.

The powerful leaders do not seek solutions to the problems. They force their will to suppress their antagonists. For example, water released from "Damodar Valley Reservoir" caused floods in South Bengal. Instead of studying for the solutions the Authorities of Bengal sealed the traffic on the Highway between Jharkhand and Bengal which was in no way connected to the problem of floods. To a larger extent we always tune to the songs of some powerful authorities and the fancy of their associates. Ironically, we feel that we were not in charge of our own life. We were not independent individuals and often live in the surroundings of helplessness.

A learned man approached a Guru for instant revelation and enlightenment The Guru advised him to stand at the City Square in the rain hands stretched and to look at the clouds in the sky. The learned man did precisely what was advised by the Guru. He came back and informed the guru that he felt like a fool. The Guru replied, "I only informed you that you would only have a revelation." It was always better to listen to our inner voice and act accordingly. Worry usually occurs, when we find our self-facing an outcome, beyond our control and so undesirable. A king lost his little finger in an accident. His close adviser well-wisher and the Minister, comforting the king said "Sir, losing a little finger was a good sign." This comment angered the king, and he banished the minister from the kingdom. The minister while leaving the kingdom said "Sir, this punishment might do some good to me "Thereafter while hunting in a forest, the king lost his way and was caught by Cannibals They intended to sacrifice the king to their Deity. They were preparing the celebrations; they were about to push him into the boiling waters. They accidently noticed that thefellow was not having his little finger and hence he was not fit for sacrifice to the Deity. An incomplete human being was not acceptable for sacrifice as per their custom. The king was saved and was set free unharmed.

On reaching safely back at his kingdom, the king realized the wisdom of his banished minister. He called him back and restored his status. The king however could not understand how the banishment was beneficial to the minster. The minister replied "Sir, I was always with you. Had you not banished me because of my comment about your little finger, I would be accompanying and with you. The cannibals would have caught me as well and as I was not having any deformity; they would have easily sacrificed me to the Deity.

It was not possible to predict precisely what would happen at a future date because we were not having all the variables at our disposal. This was exactly what happened when someone tried to assassinate Mr., Donald Trump. He was saved within One Eighth of an inch distance between him and the death. Mr. Donald Trump raised his fist, which became a fighter's symbol.

In life we were crushed like sugar cane to squeeze the juice. There were small battles fought at street corners for car parking lots. There was social conditioning, personal preferences desires to be fulfilled. People were willing to pay a lakh for a particular number license car plate. Such acts include even spiritual upliftment. There was a jagirdar who used to come on his elephant for the job. In Nizam State. Such acts isolate the individual.

Almighty becomes an internal companion for the happiness of an individual. There were a good number of enlightened souls who had the touch of Godliness during their lifetime. A story goes like this. Pandit Tulasidas had tied the Epic Rama Charit Manas in a white cloth and kept it in the temple. The temple had Four entrances. One thief wanted to steal the knotted white cloth bundle thinking it contained gold ornaments. He tried to enter the temple from one door. But he could not do so because Lord Rama was standing with His bow and arrows. He was frightened and disappointed. He tried the other door and the same disappointment. Then the Third and the Fourth same encounter. Shocked and bewildered the thief ran and fell at the feet of the saint Sri Tulsidas. The saint lifted him and embraced and said "How lucky you are. We were not able to see Lord Rama despite years of prayers"

A lightening and the accompanying thunder would not strike at the same place Twice. A man cannot be called a good person unless he got rid of hatred, pride and jealousy. Conflicts and comparisons were Society's creation and artificial. They create conflicts disharmony between individuals and between groups. We spend our energies in competition and glorify the individual or the group. We develop hatred to the extent of killing each other. We refuse to see more alternative ways of co-operation. There would be no sincere effort towards harmony. The beauty of strength in co-operation was missing. After the sporting event the people could easily rejoice together and share happiness. Trust thyself strongly and you were nearer to happiness. We were never tired so long we could see far ahead. The happiest person was he who learnt the lessons of worship. At first, we might not succeed, try again and again till you acquire happiness. The spiritual dimension was a personal area like happiness and supremely animportant one. It cannot be shared by others. We cultivate the area of faith and confidence in our self. Never give up. Confidence was a thought and a force. A good thought was more powerful than a bad one.

I give a classic example. (Times Of India 30th November 2024.) Madam Kasturi dead lifted 75Kg and squatted 55Kg in the 45 categories. Madame Kasturi Said "When I was about to lift the weight at the competition, I thought of my other lifting those bags at the railway station. Suddenly my weights felt lighter. "She won the gold medal at power lifting at the world cup in Russia. We were a product of slavery practicing pain and pleasure. We would never be living for that matter with pleasure for ever nor continuous pain. Both were having their limitations.

The wise men were forever above the crowd. Initially they might have been doubted and miss understood. Socrates, Pythagoras Copernicus, Galileo; the list was long over the generations. There was something more authentic and creative force in a human being than what meets the naked eye. The collections if you venture to record were visible and illustrative. The narrations might look disjointed because of time gaps. If our lifestyle had to change, we wanted to see that we were better placed then our attitudes must undergo a quantum change and should lead towards happiness. We must discard what was redundant. We might suffer to leave the old habits. But the sacrifice was essential, for the betterment of future life.

I give an example. There was a person in our village who was trading in chicken, eggs and hen. He lost his eyesight in an accident and became blind. Slowly he developed songs on chicken, cock fights. He used to sing in front of the houses. People used to request him to sing the songs in front of their houses and give alms in whatever fashion they could. Life must go on.

No man ever had a pride that was not injurious to him. (Burke) Animosity should not be felt against anyone. Let us not waste a single minute thinking about persons who hate us for any reason. "What the hell I was worried about. Society abhors old age. Old age seems to be the only disease into which all the diseases merges. I will continue to search for happiness. "

These were not the times of nomadic type of life where people used to hunt animals and search for fruits in the forests. These were not the times of Alaxander the Great, Ashoka Samrat or even Aurangagib, to settle the matters by swords, spears and arrows. The Mongolian Tribes played havoc, ruled ruthlessly with the help of horses. In the present-day surroundings, we were not aware who was killing whom and what for he was killing. The conflicts were visible on the screen of TV and the Satellite pictures were available in abundance. So much hatred was whipped up among the masses in a mass scale where the individual could not resist. It was a human tragedy played by the powerful leaders. The knowledge going to be discovered after a week specially in weapon, was sending shock waves. These were only strategic and logistic measures to subdue the other nation. There was no honesty of purpose. No welfare measures were involved. One pilot could easily kill or destroy a good number of people without knowing or feeling whom he was targeting. It was only useful for Statistical purpose.

We do not need any more powerful leaders in addition to the present leadership, who were tactfully managing the divisive forces of the society. These include ethnic divisions, religious conflicts boundary disputes sharing of water and other conflicts. All these generate collective hatred and mass destruction. The massages were there, but the people in Authority refuse to adhere.

(ATHARVA VEDA)

OH, MAN-Raise up from the lower levels of life. Sink not into the pit of darkness, cast away the bands, the fear of death that holds you down. Not Be frustrated in this world.

Shine like the flame of the glazing fire and glow like the radiant Sun.

Human life was like a turbulent stream strewn with rocks and pebbles. The brave soul's step into the stream. But those sitting on the bank, enumerating the hurdles shall never be able to cross the stream. Leave behind the burden of fears, guilt feeling, cumbersome attachments and inhibited weaknesses. Thus, freed from all the negative forces, smoothly cross the stream. This is happiness.

Everyone ceaselessly acts pursuing innumerable goals, ultimately directing and resulting in happiness. Happiness was a state of equilibrium with the reduction of unfulfilled desires. A man craves for objects visible to the naked eye and delighted in ownership.

I came across a person who was fighting litigations in the courts over the property matters. The knots were so cumbersome and difficult to loosen them. I asked him "Why you are smoking cigarettes. which were visibly harmful to health." He replied "What to do? I must fight these court cases. They were sitting on my nerves. I am restless. Smoking eases the tension. "I feel comfortable".

A small boy was happy winning the marbles. An elderly person was restless in the morning waiting for the Newspaper boy. For both the craving continues. For an alcoholic the absence of alcohol causes immense misery. But true happiness belongs to the nature of a man and was always personal. The kingdom of happiness lies wit in you. He who knows shall find it. That was the secret of happiness.

Sir, Bernard Shah said "Man had to face Two tragedies. One: when his desire was fulfilled and Two: When his desire was not fulfilled.

If we closely observe the cause of our unhappiness, it springs from our desires, our self-importance, and fear of contempt. The search for excellence makes us happy.

A lady after seeing Sir Bernard Shah's drama applauded its excellence. She congratulated him for producing such a masterpiece. Sir, Bernard Shah responded "Madam, within Three hours you found it excellent. It took Thirty times revision for me before I presented it on the stage.

Happiness was a probability while leading the life, but death was a certainty. Many fears were born out of helplessness and sometimes out of loneliness. But it was still a beautiful life Often we were troublesome to our self. Our unfulfilled desires make us to pull our own hair. To a man who was hungry with an empty stomach food was God. After all we live for our self. During the "Middle Ages there were sin eaters at the funeral of a departed soul. Their job was to sit by the side of the corpse take a piece of bread and eat it. By this gesture the sin eaters take away all the sins of the departed soul on their shoulders. The present generation was unlucky to that extent.

The politician declares that we were all committed for the welfare of the society. It only means that he would play the role of the leader and rest of us should serve the society. Nothing was politically right when it was ethically wrong. It was difficult for a politician to maintain integrity, where there was rampant nepotism in political hierarchy. Even a grandfather, who was occupying a seat of power, looks up fondly at his grandson who was in a cradle as a potential future leader to lead the state. After all only leaders were born only in his house. The features of leadership were already visible in the grandson. Similarly, marriages were celebrated with a grand fanfare. But living together later creates problems and all the troubles. It was no surprise that a couple living together for 25 years go for a divorce.

I quote an example. A man was accused of deserting his wife. The judge lectured him on the sins and serious consequences of deserting a wife. The judge finally asked him whether he was convinced and repenting for deserting the wife. The husband replied "Sir, My Lord, I was not a deserter. I was a refugee. It was an in Thousands, but everyone imagines that he would live for ever. (King Yudhistir's reply to Yaksha for the great wonder of the world.)

More than half of the suffering caused in the society was due to mismanagement by the Authorities at the helm of affairs. They create tensions, declare wars, displace thousands of people destroy townships, prolong the war for long periods and no cease fire. The parents who were affluent till yesterday were to run for a piece of bread to feed their children. The Authorities count their strength on the weapons they possess. Human welfare and ethics were set aside.

Problems were never unsurmountable. If the present was not capable of solving the problems and not finding workable solutions, they should hand over the reins to more meritorious Authorities. But declaring wars, ammunitions, war planes tanks and destroying shelters could in no way be treated as civilized behaviour and the welfare measure. Merit alone can open the doors for solutions. Inter dependence was more valuable than independent rulers' decisions. Even goats crossing a bridge give way to other goats coming in the opposite direction. We as human beings equipped with more intelligence could easily cope up with any situation. Smiling wins more friends than frowning.

Knowledge was based on objective realities as conceived and discovered by the Research Scholars. Ptolemy, the greatest Astronomer of Egypt, opined that Earth was the centre of the Universe. Copernicus created a paradigm shift by placing the Sun at the centre. It was impossible to change the fundamental laws of Nature. On the contrary our society was based on the visible experiences of the individuals and the co-operative norms and needs of the society. The whole functioning of the society depends on mutual co-operation. The foundations of faith and trust remain as fundamental foundations. The individual craves for liberty and freedom of the self. The conflicts in the socialfunctioning were generated by the divisive forces for keeping their identity. These were deeply rooted with selfish interests and difficult t to eradicate.

We should have faith in Dharma at collective level and Raja Dharma at governing level. People in authority need not have the approval so long they adhere these Two commandments. Assertiveness was not the wisdom. Only Truth was the assertive force. The individual need not be exposed to the hoardings on either side of the road of the governing leaders at every 100 meters Their meritorious actions should speak for themselves. After all hoardings have no life in them. They were equal to cinema posters. One man asked his friend at the funeral site of a common friend "How much he had earned?" The friend replied "I do not know! But everything he left behind. The leadership did not realize this simple truth. The carpenter's rule was measure twice but cut once. We should follow this rule for our life. These principles could not be destroyed by burning effigies, by blocking the roads or by hunger strikes until death.

We were a species for a limited period with limited dimensions. But we were blessed with intelligence and our capacity for imagination was unlimited. All these tools help us to see happiness in our life. Our problem about our life was that everyone who had a hammer in his hand thinks that every other head was a nail head, our expectations were, often our reflections of our feelings, our priorities and our individual value system. Survival was our real motivation. But the society as a unit was more powerful than the individual. It was clear that happiness was more personal and remains within the shell in the heart. It can opt be shared with others, even if we desire whole heartedly.

EIGHT
INTELLIGENCE

Spiritual dimensions were a private area in our life and difficult to share with others. Spirituality was not a product for sale, nor it could be cut in to pieces and distributed generously to people who were in but never left their names. It never occurred red to them. Similarly, the invention of the wheel was the noblest accomplishment of a man whose name we were not aware. The most profound and the most sublime experience was the sensation of the mystical awareness of the mind and the imprints it left. It was beyond our Five senses, but it was there and could not be denied. It was spiritual and so it was personal. It was related to the Soul and connected to the Almighty as explained by the Saints.

Scientific Research was objective and impersonal. They relate to physical matters like the Nature, Earth, the planets and the Universe. They were not connected to human emotions and their temperamental behaviors. Strange was the behaviour of everyone. But scientific truths were common to all humanity. Prince Saleem was born to Jodabai and Emperor Akbar after many years of "prayers. It was so recorded in the folios of History. Prince Saleem after reaching adulthood was unable to resist the bewitching glitters of Mogul Empire. He planned the death of his father and finally landed in jail. There were innumerable examples of deceit, dethroning of the kings, and coups.

Marshal TITO was the president of erstwhile nation Yugoslavia in 1950AD. He was shocked when his own Deputy President tried to over through him with the help of the Russian spies. The attempt failed and the Deputy President was arrested and jailed. Marshal TITO lamented "Whom to believe. I lifted him from an ordinary party worker to my own trusted Deputy President." The fortunes of a human being were caught between his ambitions and fulfillments.

Prejudices were a tainted product of imaginary fears, hatreds, cultivated phobias resulting in enormous sufferings. We were a bundle of likes and dislikes. Who taught us prejudices nobody knows. They relate to mob mentality and not of personal choice. Everywhere we find division, a separate identification. The Authorities formulate divisions according to the categories of convenience and present them as realities Someone shouted "Tiger, Tiger "in a village. Another person shouted "I saw the tail ". The entire village started running away from the village. No one had the patience of verifying the facts. Here the fear created by the society, created the panic. Do you believe a boy of 15 years stabbed his father because he refused to give him the key to the Two-wheeler. We were like Tennis balls. The more it hits the ground, the more it bounces back.

Spirituality comes like a flash of lightening. There was no such thing as gradual enlightenment or partial spirituality. We were obsessed with the idea of achieving something like immortality by clasping our hands in the air. The curiosity never ends. Nature on the other hand had no aims, no purpose, no goals, no fears, no wealth to safeguard, no enemies to kill. These were human attributes created by the society. The society was not orderly shaped. It was like a ship floating on the sea waters subject to the pressures of the waves and winds and always under repairs. It was like sponge dipped in water The more you squeeze the more water it would yield.

Leadership was an important machinery to organize, shape and manage the social fabric. The leadership must intelligence, wisdom, foresight and above all integrity. The leadership cannot survive without values, virtues and strength to maintain Law and Order in the society. Appointing sons' daughters and sons-in-law to the position of authority were not to be treated as virtues, wisdom or social justice and not based on integrity. Real life never works like Cinema and society was not a theater. It was difficult to catch Law Breakers who were in a position of Authority. I came across a funny slide on You Tube. A student was carrying several written slips hidden in his pant and shirt, to be used while writing the answer sheet. He also prepared one master slip like "Remote Control" to indicate which slip was placed were.

Another real incident. There was a scrap yard in a workshop which was to be sold and disposed. The lots were identified, and he would be purchaser was called to attend for negotiations before the Tender Committee, for evaluating the offer. The would-be purchaser came with a voice recorder hidden I n his coat pocket. One member said, "My daughter's marriage is fixed I need Ten

Thousand" The Second member said "Recently I purchased a Two BHK. The interior decorations are your lookout ". The Third member said "My son got admission in the college. I have to pay fees." The contractor nodded his head and walked out and left the chamber. He later handed the voice recorder to The Vigilance Authorities. Fear was a constant companion throughout our life. When we were caught in mid-stream, our first reflection would be which shore was nearer to reach.

Tragedy however painful would be eventually accepted and life continues. The other day in Isreal Air Strike nine members of a family died, leaving two survivals. None of them were a cause for this suffering and ruin. Accept the reality and the journey continues. Pray as if you were going to die tomorrow. If one imagines the invisible tiger in the forest, he would be never able to enter the forest. Do not be afraid of losing your pride status ego centricity. These were created by the society, and you believed it to be the truth.

Our serenity was buried under many forces like wealth fame addictions, social surroundings etcetera. Our energy was wasted in appeasing others. How silly it was? This sort of exercise was putting us on a mat and pushing us from the bottom by the force called invisible slavery. We were not knowing nor realizing what was the irritating port of our appeasing policies.

I came across a good number of acquaintances where I felt that the other guy was lucky. But many a time my assessment was wrong. In fact, every person was different from the other and comparisons always lead to erroneous conclusions.

One had to explore the need for prayer and meditation to realize the truth. The very cry of the elephant Gajendra caught in distress to be saved by Almighty was symbolic for the generations came afterwards. It was an involuntary effort by Gajendra to reach the invisible power of the Almighty. The elephant king of the herd, Gajendra concluded that leaning towards God was a better anchor for saving the life. There was no self-guilt. Even in pain it was better to seek the pleasure of the" Unknown". Our existence was always in the present, like that of Gajendra. Only our mind extends into future.

We do not want to remain unidentified in the society. We remain compulsive in this regard. The hoardings of the political leaders on the either side of the roads at each 100 meters distance, the advertisements of jewellery in Newspapers was a pointer in this regard. In a wedding ceremony we want to be nearer to the Bride Groom.

Once a young man enquired his neighbor: Have you seen the cinema recently released. The neighbour responded: Yes. I saw it. It was a good movie.

The young man said, you were correct. I acted in that movie. The neighbour reflecting said "But I could not remember what was your role? "Our young man replied" Sir When the criminals tied the hands and the legs of the hero, put ting him in the gunny bag and thrown him in to the river, it was I who was in the gunny bag. We always need recognition praise and compliments at any cost.

I quote another incident. We had a very strict supervisor. He was fond of directing a cinema but unfortunately, he never got an opportunity. We were a dozen clerks under his supervision. He used to shout at us for not completing the assignments in time. We had one Ansari among us. He would slowly say "Sir, have you seen the cinema recently released. The movie was nice. But in a particular scene the direction was faulty. I did not like it. Our supervisor would catch the point. He would narrate in how many scenes the direction was faulty and at places not up to the mark. Next fifteen minutes he would continue his commentary very seriously. He would forget our assignments and his discipline.

A famous boxer once refused to tie his seat belt aboard a plane. He said: Superior boxers do not need a belt.". The Air Hostess tying the belt for him replied" Sir, Superior boxers do not need a plane either "

The truly great men were those who realized the immense potentiality of a human being. They were not afraid to reveal them. The human being is of highest value on this planet. These men and women lived and adhered to truth. Killing the human beings in thousand numbers in the name of conflicts, war was a colossal waste and immense loss to human race. Intelligence and imagination were the pillars of our strength. These were instrumental to our existence and welfare.

NINE
A BUNCH OF DREAMS

Dreams come and disappear. The imprints only remain in the mind. How the dreams were formed and what they signify was beyond our comprehension. If the mind fails to capture the dream, it means that there was no dream. Dreams in a way were powerful and were a cause for surprise and could move a person. They cause pain, they cause pleasure. At times they give us happiness. and keep us cheerful. There appears to be no logical conclusions about the subject of dreams. How these dreams form was a miracle. It was for the dreamer to grasp the impressions and retain the experience if required by keeping a diary to refer later. The dream was only for the lonely person at that moment. There were no common dreams and there were no collective dreams.

Joseph, The Hebrew Youth

The dreams recorded go back to Pharaoh's regime of Egypt and narrated in the Book- THE OLD TESTAMENT

Joseph, the Hebrew youth had a dream. He told his brothers "There we were bending sheaves, in the field. Then Behold! My Sheaf arose and stood up right and indeed your sheaves stood all around and bowed down to my sheaves".

Joseph's brothers hated him even more for his dreams and his words.

The Lord was with him. Joseph was a successful youth. He was handsome in form and in appearance. He was imprecated by his master's wife. The master believed his wife and put Joseph in prison. But God showed mercy. The keeper of the jail had faith in Joseph's capacity. He gave him authority over the prisoners. It came to pass the chief Butler, and the Chief Baker offended. The pharaoh, the king of Egypt, who put them in jail. They were under the custody of Joseph, who saved them. The butler and the baker each had a dream in the night. In the morning Joseph saw both sad. Joseph enquired, "why both of you were so sad? They replied that each of them had a dream. They were no interpreters of the dreams to explain". Joseph said, do not, interpretations belong to God. Tell them to me please.

The chief butler told his dream to Joseph.

Behold, in my dream a vein was before me and in the vein, there were three branches. It budded in the blossoms shot forth its clusters brought forth the ripe grapes. Then Pharaoh's cup was in my hand. I took the grapes and pressed them into Pharaoh's cup and placed the cup in Pharaoh's hand".

Joseph said to the Chief Butler "This is the interpretation of the dream. The three branches are three days. Now within three days the Pharaoh will lift your head and restore you to your former place. You will Pharaoh's cup in his hand according to farmer manner, when you were his Chief Butler. But remember me when it is well with you. Please show kindness to me. Make mention of me to Pharaoh and get me out of this prison. For indeed I was stolen away from the land of "Hebrews. Also, I have done nothing here that they should put me into this dungeon.

When the Chief Baker heard the interpretation was good, he said to Joseph "I also saw in my dream that there were three baskets on my head. In the upper most basket there were all from finds of baked food for Pharaoh. The birds ate them out of the basket on my head.

So, Joseph answered and said "This is the interpretation of it. The Three baskets are Three days. Within Three days the Pharaoh will lift off your head from you and hang you on a tree and the birds will eat your flesh from your body."

Now it came to pass on the Third day which was Pharaoh's birthday he restored the Chief Butler to his butlership again and he placed the cup in Pharaoh's hand. Pharaoh hanged the Chief Baker as Joseph had interpreted to them. Yet the Chief Butler did not remembered Joseph and forgot him.

Pharaoh's dreams

At the end two full years, the Pharaoh had a dream" Behold! he stood by the river side. Suddenly there came out of the river seven cows, fine looking, fat and they fed in the meadow. Behold! Then there came another seven cows out of the river ugly gaunt and stood by the other cows on the bank of the river. The ugly gaunt cows ate the seven fat and fine-looking cows. The Pharaoh woke up. He slept again and dreamed a second time. Suddenly Seven heads of grain came up on stalk plumb and good. Then Behold! Seven thin heads blighted by the East wind, sprang up after them. And the seven thin heads devoured the seven plumb and full heads. And Pharaoh woke up and indeed it was a dream.

Pharaoh's spirit was troubled. He sent for all the magicians, wise men of the kingdom. The king narrated his dreams. But there was no one in the gathering, who could interpret the dreams to the Pharaoh. Then the Chief Butler spoke to Pharaoh saying "I remember my fault this day. Now there was a young Hebrew man who was with us in the prison, a servant of the captain of guards. He interpreted our dreams, and it came to pass just as he interpreted for us, and it so happened".

The Pharaoh sent the soldiers and called for Joseph. The soldiers brought Joseph from the prison and presented him before the king. Joseph was told of the dreams of Pharaoh and asked him to interpret them for the king.

Joseph answered Pharaoh saying "It is not in me. God will give an answer of peace to Pharaoh". Then Joseph told the king "The dreams of Pharaoh are one. God had told Pharaoh, what He was about to do. The seven cows are seven years. And the seven thin ugly cows which came after them are seven years. The seven empty heads blighted by the East winds are the seven years of famine. Indeed, the seven years of great plenty will come through out all the land of Egypt. But after them the seven years of famine will arise, and all the plenty will be forgotten in the land of Egypt and the famine will deplete the land of Egypt for it will be very severe.

The dream was repeated twice because the thing is established by God and God will shortly bring it to pass. Now therefore let Pharaoh select a discerning and a wise man and set him over the land of Egypt. Let Pharaoh appoint officers to collect one fifth of the produce of the land of Egypt in seven plentiful years and store up the grain under the authority of Pharaoh. Then that food shall be a reserve for the land for the seven years of famine".

Then Pharaoh said to Joseph "In as much as God has shown you all these, there is no one as discerning and wise as you."

Then Pharaoh also said, "I am Pharaoh and without your consent no man will lift his hand or foot in all the land of Egypt".

Fredrik Kekula

There were several dreams occurred even to researcher scholars and guided them to proceed further in their research.

Fredrik Kekula was a German scientist (1865AD) struggling to solve a problem in Chemistry. One-night Mr.Kekaula had a dream in which he saw a snake with its tail held within its mouth. This dream instantly put him on the right track, leading him to the solution for the perplexing question. Thus, the secret of molecular behaviour in certain organic compounds. A discovery which created a revolution in the understanding of organic chemistry.

Mr.Kekula interpreted this dream to mean that in the Benzene molecule carbon atoms bond together to form a ring structure. This knowledge gave birth to the highly developed field of synthetic molecules. (Taken from a published book).

Elias Howe

Elias Howe was the first person to mechanise the process of sewing. Through a dream, he too received the answer to a problem that had frustrated him for a long time. In his dream, he saw himself surrounded by savages threatened to kill him unless he designed a sewing machine. Being unable to respond to their demand he was tied to a tree. The savages started attacking him with spears. It surprised him to see eye lets on the spears. On waking from the dream, he immediately realised the solution which led him to invent the prototype of a sewing machine. This had dramatically revolutionised the sewing machine industry.

Lord Sri Vishnu Murty

I was struggling to record the dreams to explore the significance of dreams to the dreamer. But I failed miserably. Our responsibility lies in every act we perform. There were certain unknown factors beyond our comprehension. The dreams were one among them. The Second one was Divinity at the other extreme, These Two reflect our ignorance and no individual could share his experiences with others or convince others about their authenticity. Our life itself was full of miracles. Self-knowledge and self-experience would reveal to the mind to scale up to new heights.

I was trying hard to come out of the deep waters of the sea. The sea waters were always dark at the bottom. I saw the formation of Lord Vishnu. The full idol was slowly coming up with the face looking upwards. I was requesting the Idol not to come up as I was afraid to look at it. But the Idol slowly surfaced and was visible to the naked eye despite my resistance. It was like a man fully stretched on waters looking upwards. The idol was having four arms and a crown on its head. Fear gripped my mind.

Mahishasura Mardini

A good thought would uplift the spirit. A bad thought would dampen the spirit. One should curse himself because he had no control over the Two flows of thoughts. In the dream I saw the complete painting of " Mahishasura Mardini " on the wall in front of me. The colours were shining with Saffron covered all over from top to bottom. My first impression was a negative one. Because I was regularly chanting the full prayer daily, so it appeared in the dream. Instead of exploring the significance of the dream I took the shelter oof my own egocentrism. Later, I was ashamed of cultivating such a negative thought.

I slowly turned back to sleep. The portrait reappeared at the same spot on the wall. I was very much astonished, and the negative thought disappeared. After some time, the portrait reappeared for the Third time. This time I was fully aware of the painting on the wall and the Devi Mata's darshan. I felt that something was being conveyed to me. What it was I could not make out. The best way to keep up the happiness was to meditate and pray again and again " Mahishasura Mardini" which was possible in the waking state.

Marble Nandi

It was a dream. I was looking at a Marble Nandi standing on a Red Carpet. It was slowly floating on a velvet cloth. The Nandi was shining like a white marble and slowly rotating. I could see it in different angles. It was like a grown-up bull. Then someone prompted me to look ahead. A person was changing slides on a white sheet. The first slide was that of " Lord Shiva " Then afterwards it was followed by " Lord Ganesha" There after it was followed by another Three slides. Whom they were representing I could not make out. My spirits were lifted when I woke up.

A River

I repeat that there were many things unknown to us. The revelations of faith would not occur to us when we were in our usual senses. But the glimpses of faith were collected by the mind, when it looks inwardly. How a mind could look at a huge water sheet of a bigger size, in no time unlike a water tank we see regularly. It was formed by the flow of a river, rain or by the back waters of sea. The very sight with unending water limits and you were neck deep in the water, creates a shivering experience. I was aware that I was a good swimmer, and this thought lifted my confidence. Later, I climbed into a bus. It was running on the bridge crossing the river. Then I was whispering to the neighbour" One should not be afraid of the volume of the waterflooding at such a big she of water flowing between the banks. The fear would go away, if you stand firm. No matter if you were slapped Twice on your cheek. But fearlessness would prompt you to slap back at least once.

Lord Hanuman and Jyoti

The intention of recording the impressions was to note that the mind must be floating at a higher plane of faith and could receive the experience with and without the help of the senses. I was washing my face standing in front of the wash basin. The eyes were closed naturally. Suddenly I saw a big temple fully covered by silver plates and shing under the Sun rays. I was fully conscious of my standing posture. I was also aware that I was washing my face with the eyes closed. Seeing such a big temple bewildered me. I could not say that I was dreaming in a standing position. It was an impression formed by the mind from nowhere. Thereafter I saw Lord Hanuman on a big wallpaper of white colour. A lighted Jyoti was burning in front of Him. I was thinking how it was possible. The fact remains that I saw a vision and I was witnessing it in front of me.

Jyotis on a hill

Our attitude should be good and pure and sublime when we sit for prayer. We were living in a 100% consumer society. We were restless. No time to look at the sky and inhale a full breath to fill our lungs. Problems bang on our front door before we wake up in the morning and demand instant solutions. There were always a feeling of unfoldment and fear grips our mind. To sit and pray becomes a difficult task. One night in the dream I saw Three Jyotis lit by a mother. These Jyotis were kept on big heaps of earth. After a while the earth was removed. The Jyotis was hanging in mid-air virtually without any support. From underneath Three big monolithic mountains came up in support of these Jyotis the rocks were shining and were smooth and beautiful to look at. Someone was prompting me to look at the shining rocks and the Jyotis on each of the rock heads. Imagine how much tranquillity we gain with intense prayers. The panoramic view slowly disappeared.

Mother's Blessings

In a dream I was faithfully attached and was praying. Prayers were moral boosters. The way I was conducting myself in recent past was ridiculous and slipping into routine. I went into a temple sat in the corridor and started praying. After some time, I opened my eyes and investigated the interior of the temple. The idol of " Mata Durga Davi was completely decorated with garlands of flowers and shining jewellery. Sometime later I saw " Mata Durga Devi" in flesh and blood. A flash of light was surrounding Her full form. She was in a red colour saree. There was a shining crown on Her head. She gave me directions. I went on praying more vigorously and with more confidence.

My prayer movements included slowly in approaching nearer to Mother and seeking Her blessings. Mother was telling again and again that She would support me. I realised that I would come out of my present predicament. Off late a thought developed in my mind that prayers, reading scriptures were routine in their very nature. Peaceful way of praying became elusive. I was incapable of showing any fondness to anyone. This dream might change the course of my life in future which I needed more desperately.

Gantala Swami

In a dream I reached a hill of considerable size. The bottom layer was surrounded by a canal. The hill was located separately. There was no demarcated path to climb up to the top of the hill. We managed and reached the temple located at the top of the hill. There were a good number of people sitting in the temple premises. They were arranging the flowers and garlands. The place was lighted by oil lamps all over inside the temple. In the interior of the temple, I saw Lord Hanuman It was not very clear to see Lord Hanuman from the location where I was standing. I went nearer. The neck of Lord was decorated by carved stone bells. These bells were visible and shining. Someone standing nearby said "Lord Hanuman, Gantala Swami."

The very next day I enquired a friend whether he heard the name of" Gantala Swami." Because I never heard of" Shri Gantala Swami before. "He told me there was a temple of Lord Hanuman some 60 km. from Nandal (district) Town and was sacredly called" Ganantala Swami." I was determined to see the " Shri Gantala Swami" if luck permits, one day in future.

Trimurty

It was around 4.00AM I saw a tent on an elevated place. I was telling a person" Behold and see--From the tent Sri Rushya Singha Swami would come up" To the best of my knowledge I was not aware of any Rushi or Saint by that name, nor I came across in any book. I was astonished how I could utter that name. I was cheerfully looking towards the tent. But no Swami emerged.

After a few minutes of interval, I saw" Trimurty" slowly coming over the top of the tent. The first head was of a golden yellow colour. The head was turning and looking towards me. The middle head was of Saffron colour shining beautifully with the Sun rays directly falling on its face. It resembled " Mid-day Afternoon". The Third head was possessing that of the sky Blue. I became attentive and looking at" Tri-Murty " with reverence. Over these Three heads I saw a Five headed crown of golden colour adoring their heads.

Progress in dreams particularly could not be measured by any means. They occur and melt away. In that awareness of few minutes, we feel the eternal spirit and return to normal senses once we wake up.

Lord Shiva

I was experiencing a dream. I was wandering at the edge of a forest. I spotted a person who appeared to be a normal person, like me. As I was slowly moving towards him and the distance reduced, he appeared to be a saintly person. His body was covered fully by a saffron cloth. He signalled me to come. I was attracted towards him instinctively. I followed him into the forest. I developed fear. The big trees were stretching their shadows on the ground. As we were walking on the fallen dry leaves, we were listening to the sounds of some things were moving and hiding under the leaves. The saint told me to wait. He would go to Lord Shiva's temple and return. There was no sufficient light and the forest was thick. The surroundings were covered by darkness.

I developed some courage and slowly investigated the interior of the temple. I saw a full Six feet Idol of Lord Shiva in a black granite stone standing on a pedestal. There were a good number of snakes stirring on the ground under the fallen dry leaves. The sounds frightened me. I made swift move, pulled some leaves from a nearby branch of a plant and with a gesture of prayer thrown the leaves on the Idol in the temple. These leaves happen to be " Tulasi Leaves "which were considered as sacred and dearer to Lord Shiva. I saw Lord Shiva with full satisfaction in the interior of the temple. I quickly moved away from the place before any of those snakes could catch up with me. The saint had come back and said he had thrown away the bunch of the snakes and prayed to " Lord Shiva "All these movements were taken with full awareness. At one stage the saint was caught by a snake. I had to pull it away by force before it could do any harm. I was not able to understand the significance of this dream.

Destiny

This was a strange dream. I was convinced that there was a lingering link which we were not able to fully comprehend with those who had expired in front of our very eyes. That was not the end of it. Mind was the real instrument through which the link was laid, and we were able to experience, pertaining to that subtle area. Today in the afternoon I was resting after meals. I had a dream. The dream escapes our perceptions and our senses. We could recall the incidents which occurred some decades back. We were inclined to call it the memories of the memory lane, where those were stored. We were making them to stand before us in seconds. The reflections with the departed souls were parallel and like those memory lanes but the only difference was the promptings come from the departed souls and not volunteered by our minds.

I saw my younger brother in the dream. He had expired Three years back. I started talking to him. He was cheerful and enquiring about the welfare of the other family members. How were they? I was at Bengaluru. Our conversation was taking place at his own house at Secunderabad. Some renovation work was going on in his house. He said " Let us move out and go elsewhere. The cement smell was not good." We moved out through another door into a hall.

Why so much explanation? I was eager to establish the sequences connected to this dream. After a week I happened to visit Secunderabad, In the interval period I had another dream. I was travelling in the bus. The bus was crossing the river. The bridge was long, and the river was with full of water flow. On reaching the other bank of the river I got down from the bus. I saw my brother's son was waving his hand from a distance. He had an envelope in his hand. It looked that he had some message to convey through the envelope.

Keeping these Two dreams in my mind I wanted to conduct a " Family Get Together" at my brother's house. It was not possible to conduct the function at his house because of the renovation work, replacement of tiles. I wanted to satisfy my departed brother' soul. I tried to persuade another nephew to arrange the " Get Together". But he later backed out. All the family members were against the " Get Together" They were in one voice ridiculed my plan and criticised my conducting the party.

I never revealed my dreams and become a laughingstock. Finally, it so happened we have conducted the " Get Together" at the residence of my brother' son. We were happy. All came with the short notice at us dis postal. We spent the full day cheerfully. My brother's son was the same fellow who waved the envelope when I got down from the bus in the other dream. During our conversations again the topic of hurry burry arrangement of " Get Together " came and I was subjected to criticism. I was sure the soul of my departed brother must have remained with us and was satisfied. The other members of the party again put me on the mat and said how illogical and unreasonable I was in insisting and forcing the " Get Together". I was not able to withstand the criticism further I narrated the dreams I had. I was not aware of the renovation work going on in my brother's house. In my dream I visited their house along with my brother and the conversation I had with him and the envelope I received from his son. I said, " Finally we landed in my brother's son's house for which I got the invitation beforehand. "All went well without solving how such dreams occur and indicate the future events. It becomes a wonder after the event.

Flying Eagle

If we were afraid of anyone or anything, there would be no happiness. When we were in solitude mood and do not admit fear, then suddenly a strange thing happens uninvited which we may call it as love, Truth or Happiness. (J. Krishna Murty)

I was struggling with back pain. I lacked the firmness of the steps and was careful in the bathroom. With all this I ventured to move out to see " Flower Exhibition " at Lalbagh. It was a unique show of flowers. Around 3.5 lakh flowers were collected all over the Globe and were arranged for the exhibition. It was there for 10 days. The flowers were kept afresh by covering with a moisture dome. Every year the " Flower Show" was dedicated to some famous personality. This time (January 2024) it was in the name of " Saint Basananna "the social reformer of Twelfth Century. This exhibition was a unique speciality of Bengaluru city.

Around 04.00 AM I had a dream. I entered a big area. There was a big heap of stones. My job was to cut these big stones into small rectangular pieces and collect the wages in the evening and leave the place. After arranging the rectangular pieces in an orderly manner, I was about to leave. All the pieces suddenly turned into red colour. I was trying to locate my position. I was in the same bed. After all a dream was a dream only.

I saw an eagle was flying in the air above the mountain top and was coming in my direction. Someone was shouting " The eagle was for you. receive it ". The eagle was young and energetic with shineing green feathers under its neck. I got up went down into the open space to receive the bird. I stretched my hands and received the eagle and hugged it. I woke up and it was 04.00 AM. I got up from the bed. surprisingly the back pain was completely reduced. I felt the relief and came back to almost normalcy. The question disturbing my mind was whether a dream could cure our illness as well.

Wall Posters

It was around 03.30 AM. Neither I was sleeping well, nor I was willing to get up from the bed. I started chanting the name of Lord Shiva with a powerful determination. It continued and no

stop was visible. The mind with all its immense capacity was a timid organ. If you let it lose it would create several thoughts. I was not able to stop the chanting the name of Lord Shiva. Sometime later I slept.

In front of me there appeared a completely blank wall. Some wall posters started coming one after another. Each one was different from the next one that followed. I was not able to identify whether the posters were of " Mata Kanaka Durga, Mata Bala Tripura Sundari, Mata Annapurna or Mata Madhura Minakshi. I started seeing the wall posters closely. These wall posters continued to appear for some time.

Then I saw some people were moving swiftly. But why I was not able to reach the Temple though I was standing in the queue. Then slowly at a distance I saw Lord Ganapati decorated by shining diamonds. Lord Ganesha was crowned on a decorated elephant. The reflection of the Sun rays on the diamonds made the decorations more shining.

I was happy that despite not able to move in the queue, I was able see Lord Ganesha to my satisfaction. Suddenly I was thinking, " Why I was not able to see any Deity inspite of chanting vigorously Lord Shiva 's name. Later, I saw Four Brass plates, on which images of Gods were nicely carved. Behind these plates I saw on a lengthy marble bench. There were 7 to 8 marble Idols of Gods arranged skillfully standing one after another in a horizontal row shining brightly in white colour. In the background a thick yellow paper was projected. I thought that I should shift the entire table to my room. Later, I realised that there was not sufficient place in my room to keep such huge set up. I dropped the idea. I woke up.

So many Godly figures in one dream was a good experience. Where it takes us and how it takes us, I was not capable of knowing.

Lord Hanuman

God's blessings come in its own accordance. How it comes and why it comes was outside the scope of our wildest imagination. These were the gestures, some intimations significant to the dreamer, which perhaps passes through the dream media and touches the mind. These experiences were not the creation of the mind. They were neither wilful illusion. The only rational conclusion would be that there were certain destinies unknown to the dreamer.

Today I was sitting in a hall attending a conference along with others, most of them were strangers. A good number of voices and notices were vibrating in the conference hall, but there was no clarity. I came out, got into a bus to reach the lodge, where abouts were not known to me. It was a confused bus travel for a good length

While I was looking through the window, some lady was giving Arati to " Davi Mata" Mata sat on an elevated semicircular pedestal in the courtyard of the house. A Neem tree was there, most covering the roof top of the house. All the walls of the house were decorated by Yellow Turmeric paint. There was Saffron circular Bindus at regular interval distances of One Foot between Two Bindus. It was some devotee's house. The Arti started after completion of "Pooja " and the prayer song was audible to me, sitting in the bus. It was interesting to see the absolute devotion of the family members including children.

The bus was in slow motion. Next to the house, I saw " Lord Hanuman's bust in a floating motion in the air with an outstretched Right Hand. On the palm of the outstretched hand the replica of the Green Mountain was placed. The Sanjeevini plant was being carried to save the life of " Sri Laxmana Dava". The " Gadapani " was in the grip of left hand raised. The bust of Lord Hanuman was also fully decorated and covered by Turmeric paint. The Saffron Bindus was there at regular distances of One foot, like those of the devotes house. Who did these paintings, of course not known to me. How many days it took for them for painting the devotes house and the adjacent " Lord Hanuman's Bust? The Lord Hanuman's bust could be touched by stretching the hand through the window of the bus. The sight had its sublime effect on me. The bus moved ahead leaving the bust of " Lord Hanuman" behind. I woke up and sat on the cot for a good length of time.

Light Humour

The father said: My son, after my death if you find it difficult to lead your life in this village and decide to go elsewhere for livelihood, please do me a favour. Remove the dilapidated wall of our courtyard and depart. It was built by own hands. I do not want it uncared for.

Later, one day the son finally decided to leave the village. He also dreamt that he was going to the nearby village to seek the advice of his friend about his plans. The next day he went and told his friend about his plans to leave the village. He also informed him about the dream he had.

The friend laughed and said: You came all the way to seek my advice because you had the dream. How foolish you were? I too had a dream like you. I was digging that dilapidated wall in your house, but I did not rush to your village and started digging that wall.

The friend thanked him and left back to his village. He remembered his father's wish. He dug out the wall. To his utter surprise and shock he saw a box hidden underneath containing gold coins.

TEN
CLOUDS SPEAK

We were on a pilgrimage to Bhadrachalam, in the last week of July month. The TV channels were showing floods in Godavari River. The waters were touching the temple premises. All the approachable routes were blocked except the National Highway from Vijayawada to the Temple town. People were advised not to take the risk of travelling. It was the position on 23.07.2023. On that day around 04.00AM I had a dream. From a distance I was seeing the Idol of Sri Rama. It was the first time in my life I could see the Idol of Sri Rama in the dream. He was standing at the Temple premises, the Gopuram was visible in the background. The temple was at an elevated place on a hillock. The Idol was in the light sky-blue colour, with the mixture of the ripened Leman fruit colour. The Sun rays were falling, and the Idol was shining in the midnoon.

The Idol was at a distance and continue to appear now and then. I was travelling along with some devotes. Enroute some more devotes climbed into the bus. A huge Black cloud with its silver lining at the edges was moving in the sky in the same direction of our bus. I went on observing this huge cloud moving towards Sri Ram's temple. I was pointing out to the other devotes," See. This cloud was also moving to worship Sri Rama. How could a cloud move to worship the Lord? The very thought surprised me! For me clouds were meant to give rains only. I ever heard the clouds were being named was " Megha Sandesam ".

The cloud started talking to me It said, " We were also going to Bhadrachalam to worship Lord Rama." It was a shock of my life. How a cloud was having its own mind and a vocabulary to communicate. It was telling me to join them and pray to Sri Rama". I requested all the devotes to get down from the bus and form a circle and sit. We formed a circle on the bank of river

" Godavari ". We started Bhajans included in Lord Rama's name. The nearby flood waters were roaring and were frighting us. Even to look at the current of flood water was creating fear in our spinal cords.

After 30 minutes we climbed back into the bus and moved on the road in the direction of the temple. On reaching the temple I looked up to see, whether the cloud also reached the Temple to worship Lord Sri Rama. The dream faded away. I prayed that I should never forget this dream.

A cloud was a huge water filter. It purifies the salt water of the sea. It also functions like a big water tanker carrying water to different destinations, without collecting any transport charges. It spreads water to vast areas free of labour charges. If there were no clouds, no rain, no rivers, no farming and no grains. Humans might have perished long back.

We should do "Arati" to these clouds as we were doing Aarati at Kashi and Hari Dwar to Mata Ganga River. All of us should maintain a diary, record our dreams and exchange our experiences. Why we should not pray and give our gratitude to these clouds. I do not know why our ancestors had not submitted their prayers as a gratitude to the clouds as they did for SUN, Rivers as a part of Nature's gifts to humanity.

ELEVEN
PAIN AND PLEASURE

The secret of modern life was time management. The most valuable commodity in urban city environment was time. In case we must develop into future as independent individuals and all so build up a welfare society, we must ration out all consumable items including Time. Time was related to individual's existence. He had to make provision of Time:

1. *To cover the distance between residence and workplace*
2. *to adjust for traffic jams*
3. *for checking e- mails, important and unimportant*
4. *staring into mobile screens being a bulk commodity,*
5. *TV channels for News, matches, serials and cinemas,*
6. *You- Tube*
7. *Curtesy calls, etc. Etc.*

It was important to measure how efficient and effective we were in saving Time rather than managing Time. The universal feeling of having too much to do but did not have enough Time was a daily reality. The mobile phone occupies our Time while waiting for Two/Three minutes for the lift was a proof in connection with the Time.

A saint advised a Delhi's citizen " My dear, spare some time for prayers and meditation. "Apt came the reply " Babajee, I do not have time to die. you are advising me to do prayers and meditation."

Life was a long-distance marathon race. We need to plan and phase our activities to fulfil our desires:

1. *Meet the targets imposed,*

2. *keep a healthy state of body and the mind,*
3. *reduce the feeling of the pressure of lack of Tme,*
4. *4.rest and sufficient Time to sleep*
5. *reduce anxieties, despair and the attitude of depression.*

The remedy lies in making the life simple. Stay for a while and question your own life:

My old college, who had crossed 92 years kept a list of mobile numbers in a diary. He instructed his son, to inform those people whenever his death occurs. A novel way of conducting one's own obituary announcement. This fact, I was not aware.

I had a dream in which a lady informed me that my erstwhile colleague was in " ICU " and his survival was doubtful. She said, " I took your number from my brother's diary ". After an interval of about 30 minutes, another sister took the phone and said "Uncle sorry for the information conveyed earlier by my sister. As per doctor's latest version my brother was improving and he was out of danger, there was no need for panic. The dream ended there.

I was shocked. All the memories came to surface and troubled me. The very next week I went to Chennai to see him. His sister told me exactly what she conveyed in the dream. She also said that she got my mobile number from his diary. My friend was improving. It was a fact that he was under "ICU". The point we were discussing was the capacity of a resource hidden in a human being. How the mind worked as a receiver? How strange was the communication? Who conveyed and who corrected the information? Who received it in the dream? Honestly, we must accept our ignorance. These communications were beyond our sense organs. Mind was the only link to connect and convey the contents.

In a dream I was loitering on the footpath at Parel in Mumbai. I spotted my Ex-Boss under whom I worked for 8 years. I left the job 5 years back. There was no communication later. He was stationed at Mumbai, and I was at Bengaluru. Along with him I entered a big hall. I saw Two corpses laid side by side. Each one was of Ten Feet in length and were fully covered by bandage cloth of White colour commonly used in the hospitals. Someone told my Ex-Boss" The corpse on the right side belongs to him. He could take it away. Before that he had to sign certain documents in the court in front of a judge.

I saw him coming to the Court with the documents in hand. He started signing the documents I witnessed his signature as I was familiar with it. Then he invited me to visit his new office in the afternoon. The dream finished and I woke up. In the morning, I took the trouble of typing the entire dream and sent it on " Words App" to his mobile as a fancy item. The intention was to revive the contact. With in 10 minutes, I got the response. He thanked me for the narration of the dream. He said" I was about to leave the house, to go to the Court to sign the legal documents in the presence of a judge. These relate to a settlement of a dispute between him and a " Japanese Corporation". He also confirmed that he had opened a new office and invited me to visit while in Mumbai etc. "

All these developments were not known to me, since there was no communication for the last 5 years. The point at issue was which was that source gave me all the information? Where was the need to give that information? Once more it was proved that there were certain instruments or tools lying in our domain. They were beyond our capacity to grasp and know the source. We have no command over them. They appear and disappear. In fact, at the risk of being laughed and ridiculed I requested my friends to maintain a diary of dreams and explore as a research item.

The Third dream was equally funny, and no logic would reach any conclusion. It was around 04.30 AM of 6th November 2024. I was pushed into a hall where a group of people were sitting. None of them were having shirts. It was a Cabinet Hall in the White House-Washington DC. In the sitting posture no one was having anything to wear above the belt. I felt elated. Probably they were going to offer me a status and responsibility to perform. I noticed Mr. Donald Trump was also sitting without a shirt, at an arm's distance from me. Mr. Donald Trump got up and trying to walk. He was faltering in his steps and about to fall. I stretched my hand to support him and preventing him from falling. Someone was shouting 80% over and only 20% was left. Mr. Donald Trump was exactly Two feet above the ground level. I saved him from touching the ground.

I woke up and wondering what the dream was conveying. When other members of the family got up from their respective beds. I declared that Mr. Donald Trump won the presidential elections. Afterwards on 6th November 2024 the entire world came to know of the results. Where was Bengaluru where was Washinton DC? What was the significance? Who gave me the privilege to enter the Cabinet Hall in White House? It was a momentary status given to me and I enjoyed it in my dream.

One of the best strategies to channel the energy positively was to think the welfare of others. This will help to shift from isolation and loneliness. It was hard to nurture negative thoughts, when we were feeling grateful and wanted to express our gratitude.

Science explores the existence of objects and physical world. These relates to life less matters. On the other hand, the individuals were empowered by intelligence and unlimited imagination. Even children were gifted with these emotional aspects at the time of their birth. But majority of the people were sucked in to the society and lose their self and power to explore their own capacities. They reveal their fears of failures at every second step which were the creation of social environment and not related to the emotional aspects of the person. The society never speaks for the individuals and always upholds the stronger elements and condemns the weak lings and becomes quite gullible.

We were the rulers of our own existence and the destiny we cherish and the happiness we generate. We were not born to kill each other. We were not born to hate others and emotionally harm them.